The Pet Shop Revolution

ANA JUAN

ARTHUR A. LEVINE BOOKS
AN IMPRINT OF SCHOLASTIC INC.

Mr. Walnut owned the biggest pet shop in the city.
But everyone was afraid of him.

He always had a terrible scowl on his face,
with smoldering eyes and a deep, deep frown.

Mr. Walnut's pet shop was dark and cold.

He sold all kinds of animals — big, small, wild, timid . . . all different,
but they all looked out of their small steel cages with sadness in their eyes.

No one knew Mr. Walnut well. And, in fact, he kept a big secret: He wore a wig to hide his shiny bald head. Every morning he combed and combed it, shaping and fluffing so no one would be able to tell it wasn't real. "If anyone knew," he grumbled, "I would die of embarrassment."

Then every night, he put his wig on a monkey caged in his room and combed it for hours. If a hair fell loose, he plucked one from the poor monkey's tail to replace it.

Mina lived a few doors down from the pet shop. Every day she heard the neighbors complain about the bad smell and terrible cries of the unhappy animals, but no one was brave enough to complain to the terrifying owner.

The only people Mina saw enter the store were rich customers from out of town.
And Bobo, a local boy who delivered ice for the penguins. Bobo always went into
the shop whistling and smiling, but he came out heartbroken, his shoulders drooping.

One day, after Bobo delivered the ice, he found Mina on the bridge.

"What are you doing here?" asked Bobo.

"I am looking for my rabbit, Mimi. Today when I woke up she wasn't
in her cage. I'm sure Mr. Walnut has Mimi and I want her back!!!"

"You're a brave girl, Mina." Bobo said.
"I have an idea. Listen. . . ."

Next day, Bobo delivered the ice as usual.

"Mr. Walnut," he said. "I'm afraid the price has gone up."

"What??!!!" shouted Mr. Walnut.
"That's outrageous!!!"

And while they argued, Mina jumped out of the ice trolley.

Night came over the city.

Mina waited until Mr. Walnut put his wig on the monkey and went to sleep.

When he started to snore, Mina opened the cages
and led the animals in silence to the main door.

Once the animals were all together, Mina opened the door and they ran in a great stampede of fur and feathers across the rumbling bridge.

The racket woke Mr. Walnut, and he ran to the window. "Aaaaah!" he screamed, reaching for his coat and keys. But something felt funny. Before he opened the door, he reached for his head, and then he screamed even louder.

Where was his wig???? Without it, he could never leave the house!!

Mina, Bobo, and the animals listened to Mr. Walnut howl with rage inside the empty shop. Mina hugged her rabbit, and Bobo jumped around the happy animals. Gradually, the neighbors came out to join them.

All that day, Mr. Walnut shouted out his window, but he wouldn't leave the house without his wig. He could only watch the party outside.

By sundown, Mr. Walnut was desperate and hungry.
"Please come back!" he wailed piteously. "I'm hungry!!!
I always fed you all very well, and now you've forgotten meeeee . . . !!!"

Fed up with his yelling, Mina and Bobo and the animals decided to bring some food to Mr. Walnut. Bobo carried the meal on his trolley and waited near the pet shop.

Quickly, the door opened a crack, and the giraffe pushed the food inside.

Days passed, and Mr. Walnut grew sadder and quieter. Sometimes, he climbed to the shop's watchtower and, through binoculars, spied the animals enjoying the city. He longed to catch them again so everything would go back to the way it was.

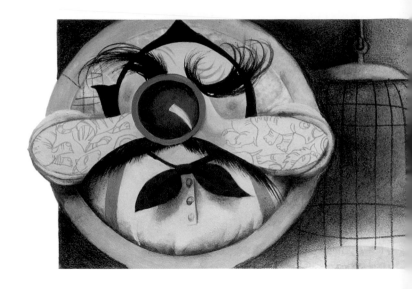

But his vanity was stronger than his longing. So without his wig he was still trapped inside. The pet shop became his cage.

Even the phone stopped ringing.

One day, he was struck with an idea. "Now I know how to get my pet shop back!!!" he cried.

Immediately he set to work, looking for old sacks, straw, ribbons, wire. . . . Every once in a while he would go to the window and stare as before. But this time he made notes and sketched ideas on a pad. His activity was hectic. He didn't sleep. Food lay untouched outside the pet shop door. And the shop was eerily quiet.

The neighbors met with Mina and Bobo and the animals.
"Is he up to something?" Mina worried.
"Is he sick?" Bobo wondered.

Carefully they crossed the bridge and got closer to the pet shop. From the window they could see Mr. Walnut sawing and clipping, sewing and gluing, surrounded by mountains of plush toys . . . toys that looked more than a little familiar. . . !

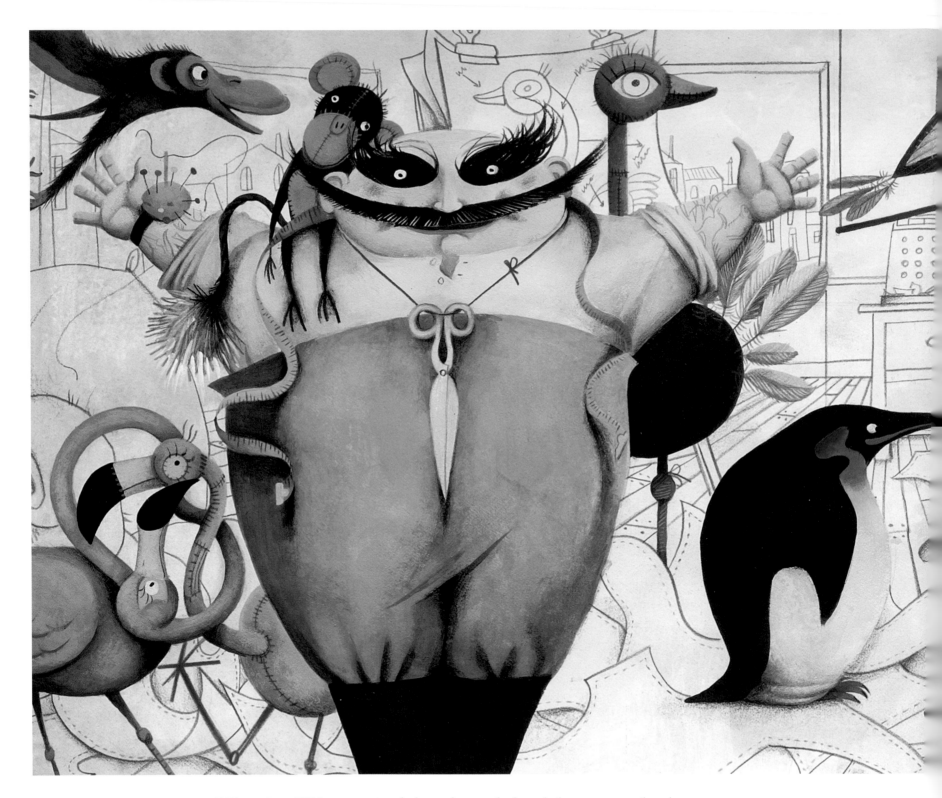

When Mr. Walnut noticed them he smiled and threw open the door.
"Welcome! Welcome!" he said. "Would you all like to help me?"

And so, the once dark pet shop became a big, bright toy factory.

The animals posed, cut, and sewed. The cages were
thrown out to make room for shelves and tables.

And the rich clients came back to buy plush versions of the animals they once wanted to own. Mr. Walnut was so busy that he even forgot about his wig.

But the monkey sometimes lent his tail on special occasions.

Of course, Mr. Walnut still kept everyone awake with his snoring.
But that's another story.

To Matz

All rights reserved. Published by Arthur A. Levine Books, an imprint of Scholastic Inc.,
Publishers since 1920. SCHOLASTIC and the LANTERN LOGO are trademarks
and/or registered trademarks of Scholastic Inc.

LIBRARY OF CONGRESS CATALOGING-IN-PUBLICATION DATA

Juan, Ana.
The pet shop revolution / Ana Juan.—1st ed.   p.   cm.
Summary: Everyone is afraid of Mr. Walnut, the scowling owner of the biggest pet
store in the city, who sells all kinds of animals to rich customers from out of town,
but when Mina's pet rabbit goes missing she vows to do something about it.
ISBN 978-0-545-12810-0 (hardcover : alk. paper) [1. Pet shops—Fiction.
2. Animals—Fiction. 3. Animal rescue—Fiction.
4. Pride and vanity—Fiction.] I. Title.
PZ7.J8575Pe 2011   [E] —dc22   2010051325

10 9 8 7 6 5 4 3 2 1   11 12 13 14 15

First edition, October 2011

Printed in Singapore   46

The text was set in Adobe Garamond Pro.
The display type was set in Ziggy ITC and Windsor BT.
The art for this book was created using acrylics and colored pencils on paper.

Art direction and book design by Marijka Kostiw